Puffin Books

SingenPoo
Shoots Through

Singenpoo* wanted me to follow.
She had written a sign the only way she could.
What a relief. What a cat.

Singenpoo does a disappearing act.
And she might not be back.

Muddles, puddles and pee.
From the wacky, wild world
of Paul Jennings.

* Singenpoo is a weird name. But then
  Singenpoo is a weird cat. You can read
  more about her in *The Paw Thing* and
  Singenpoo Strikes Again.

Other books by Paul Jennings

Unreal
Unbelievable
Quirky Tails
Uncanny
Unbearable
Unmentionable
Undone
Uncovered
Unseen
Round the Twist

The Cabbage Patch Fib
The Cabbage Patch War
(illustrated by Craig Smith)

The Paw Thing
Singenpoo Strikes Again
(illustrated by Keith McEwan)

The Gizmo
The Gizmo Again
Come Back Gizmo
Sink the Gizmo
(illustrated by Keith McEwan)

Wicked!
(with Morris Gleitzman)

SingenPoo Shoots Through

Paul Jennings

Illustrated by
Keith McEwan

PUFFIN BOOKS

Puffin Books
Penguin Books Australia Ltd
487 Maroondah Highway, PO Box 257
Ringwood, Victoria 3134, Australia
Penguin Books Ltd
Harmondsworth, Middlesex, England
Penguin Putnam Inc.
375 Hudson Street, New York, New York 10014, USA
Penguin Books Canada Limited
10 Alcorn Avenue, Toronto, Ontario, Canada, M4V 3B2
Penguin Books (N.Z.) Ltd
Cnr Rosedale and Airborne Roads, Albany, Auckland, New Zealand
Penguin Books (South Africa) (Pty) Ltd
5 Watkins Street, Denver Ext 4, 2094, South Africa
Penguin Books India (P) Ltd
11, Community Centre, Panchsheel Park, New Delhi —110 017, India

First published by Penguin Books Australia, 1999
10 9 8 7 6 5 4 3 2 1
Copyright © Lockley Lodge Pty Ltd, 1999
Illustrations copyright © Keith McEwan, 1999

Designed by George Dale, Penguin Design Studio
Typeset in 12$^{1}/_{2}$/15 Palatino by Midland Typesetters, Maryborough, Victoria
Made and printed in Australia by The Australian Book Connection, Victoria

National Library of Australia
Cataloguing-in-Publication data:

Jennings, Paul, 1943– .
Singenpoo shoots through.

ISBN 0 14 130609 2.

1. McEwan, Keith. II. Title.

A823.3

www.puffin.com.au

To Kyle and Sage – P.J.
To my father, Hugh McEwan – K. M.

'Brilliant,' I said to my cat Singenpoo. 'Well done.'

Singenpoo didn't seem to hear. She had her paw on the mouse and she wasn't taking it off.

'ELEPHANT,' yelled out a kid in the crowd.

Singenpoo clicked on the word ELEPHANT and the computer played a little tune. The crowd clapped loudly. 'Good girl,' I whispered.

'BANANA,' shouted an old lady.

Singenpoo gave a small purr and clicked the mouse again. The word BANANA lit up on the screen and the jingly tune filled the air. The crowd went wild. They had never seen a cat that could read before.

'That's all, folks,' said The Boss. 'That's the end of the show for today.'

The audience stood up and started to file out of the tent. The Boss put a hand on my shoulder. 'Good stuff, Scott,' he said. 'The crowd loves your act. You're hired. You and the cat.'

I grinned and stroked Singenpoo's fur. A Christmas act in a carnival. Terrific. Much better than my last job at Major Mac's take-away chicken shop. I couldn't go back there after he was so mean to Singenpoo. I just hoped my new boss was going to be better.

'Thanks a million,' I said to The Boss. 'This job means a lot to me. I need the money because Mum is on the pension and we're behind with the rent.'

'You've got a good act,' said The Boss. 'A cat pretending to read. It's a great trick. And those glasses are a terrific touch.'

'Thanks,' I said. 'But it's not a trick. Singenpoo can read as well as I can. And the glasses are real. She needs them for the small print.'

The Boss gave a loud laugh. 'Don't give me that,' he said. 'Cats can't read. I know a fake act when I see one. Which reminds me. Come and meet Felicity.' He took me into the next tent and pointed at a large water tank.

'She's a fake as well,' said The Boss.

'Wow,' I said. 'She looks real.'

She did too. Felicity's hair was long and fair. And her tail sparkled like a fish with wet scales. She sure seemed genuine to me.

The Boss chuckled to himself. 'Of course she looks real. No one is going to pay to see a mermaid if she looks phoney.'

'She can even move her tail,' I said. 'How does she do that?'

'You tell me the trick to your cat,' said The Boss, 'and I'll tell you the trick to The Mermaid.'

'Singenpoo *can* read,' I yelled. 'Singenpoo is not a fake. There is no trick.'

The Boss laughed. 'Fair enough,' he said. 'You keep your secrets if you want to.'

He gave a sign to Felicity
The Mermaid and she slipped
out of her tank and flopped
around on the floor.

Singenpoo gave a little meow
and licked her lips. She couldn't
take her eyes off The Mermaid.

'It's not a fish, Singenpoo,'
I said. 'It's not even a
mermaid really.'

'This is Scott and Singenpoo,' The Boss said to Felicity. 'They are our new act.'

Felicity quivered and waved her tail around. Singenpoo crouched like a hunter. Oh no. I knew what that meant. I tried to stop her.

'Singen . . .' I yelled. Too late.

She pounced on The Mermaid's tail with her claws out and gave it a nip. She bit right into the rubber tail and tried to chew.

Felicity screamed. 'Get her off me,' she yelled.

I reached down and grabbed Singenpoo. Felicity reached down and unzipped her tail. She pulled it right off and scrambled to her feet. The rubber fishtail lay still and lifeless on the floor of the tent.

Poor Singenpoo started to shake. She was scared out of her wits by the strange sight of The Mermaid ripping off its tail.

'I'm sorry,' I said. 'But Singenpoo thought you were food. She just couldn't help herself.'

Felicity hitched up her bikini and stared at Singenpoo. A sad look came over her face. 'Pets should be kept locked up,' she said. 'Where they can't do any harm.' Then she turned and walked off towards her caravan without another word.

'Don't worry about it,' said The Boss. 'It gets cold swimming around in that tank all day. It makes her miserable. Come on, I'll show you where you are going to live.'

I picked up Singenpoo and gave her a rub. 'It's okay, girl,' I said. 'I'll look after you. No one will ever come between us, no matter what.'

The Boss showed us around the carnival. There were lots of acts and side-shows – a fire-eater, a volcano blowing out balls with lucky numbers on them, knock 'em downs, a rocket to Mars, dodgem cars, about six rides including the Mad Mouse and the Jaws of Death. There was also an elephant, a juggling dog and a two-headed rabbit.

'The rabbit is a fake,' said The Boss. 'But the elephant is real.'

'You're joking?' I said. I was disappointed that so many of the acts were fakes. Not like Singenpoo. I couldn't wait to show the next crowd what she could do.

The Boss took us around the back of the tents to the performers' caravans. We walked past one with a mermaid painted on the side. I knew who that belonged to. The door suddenly opened and a man stepped out.

Not a woman. Not a mermaid. A very sad-looking man. He glanced our way and started to shuffle off. Singenpoo began to purr. She seemed very interested in him.

'Oh-oh,' said The Boss. 'Jack's out. This means trouble.'

Felicity's face appeared at the van door. 'Jack,' she yelled in a loud voice. 'Come back here.'

The poor guy stopped dead in his tracks. At first I thought he was going to run for it. But he slowly made his way back to the caravan. He looked so unhappy as he disappeared back into the van with Felicity.

'Poor old Jack,' said The Boss.
'He gets the wanders.'

The Boss showed us our van. A beat-up old thing with paint peeling off and cracks in the window. 'Get a good night's sleep,' he said as we made our way inside.

The van was very small but it was home. I was excited about living with the carnival people. 'This is just the start,' I said to Singenpoo. 'You and I will make a lot of money for Mum.'

Singenpoo didn't seem to be listening. She was looking out the window at Felicity's van. And there was the man inside staring back. He had the saddest eyes I had ever seen. They seemed to be saying, 'Help. Please help.' Suddenly Felicity appeared next to him at the window. She looked across at us and closed the curtains.

'There's something not quite right going on in there,' I said to Singenpoo. I started to worry. Why was a grown-up being treated like a little kid?

Singenpoo jumped out of the window without a purr and went off to explore. I closed the curtains and started to cook tea. Tomorrow we would be performing for the whole day and I had to get to bed early. It would be our first real day working at the carnival and I didn't want anything to go wrong.

2

A loud scream woke me the next morning. A terrible high-pitched shriek. I pulled on my clothes and headed out of the door. 'Come on, Singenpoo,' I yelled. 'Something's wrong.'

Singenpoo scrambled under the bed. She didn't want to come.

I started to get worried. Singenpoo seemed to know something that I didn't. Why was she so frightened? I reached under the bed, grabbed her trembling body and hurried past Felicity's van. The same scared, lonely face was looking out. What was going on? Who was that man?

This wasn't the time to find out. I hurried past the juggler's stand and the fairy-floss seller towards the main tent where the scream had come from. A group of clowns were poking their heads inside the tent, laughing. How could they be laughing when someone was screaming in terror?

I soon found out.

Felicity stood there beside her tank holding her rubber mermaid's tail and shrieking at the top of her voice. She wasn't frightened. She wasn't hurt. But she *was* very upset.

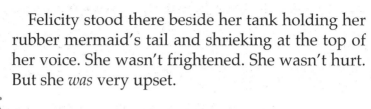

'Yuck,' she shouted at The Boss. 'That is foul.'

Singenpoo was shivering in my arms.

'It's that cat,' she said. 'It's weird.'

'What?' I said. 'She hasn't done anything.'

The Boss pointed at The Mermaid's water tank. Three little brown things were bobbing around on the surface.

'The cat has polluted my tank, that's what,' said Felicity. 'I'm not swimming in that.'

I looked closely. Oh no. Oh yes. Three pieces of cat poo were floating on top of the water. I could tell by the colour and shape that they belonged to Singenpoo. I would have known them anywhere.

'Singenpoo,' I said. 'How could you? Why did you?'

My mind flashed back to the time Singenpoo peed in Major Mac's wine. But that was different. He deserved it. He was a mean man. He lied and cheated. But Felicity hadn't done anything to us. Why didn't Singenpoo like her?

'Bad girl,' I said to Singenpoo.

Singenpoo hissed and then jumped out of my arms and shot out of the tent.

She scampered across to Felicity's caravan and meowed. The man with the sad face looked out of the window. When he saw Singenpoo his eyes lit up with pleasure. Why was he so fond of my cat? Singenpoo scratched at the door and meowed again. She was trying to tell us something.

'Who is that guy?' I asked.

'We call him Silly Jack,' said The Boss. 'He sweeps up and does the dishes for Felicity.'

I felt sorry for Jack. He wasn't allowed out and he had to do all the yucky jobs. Singenpoo sure liked him. I started to feel a bit jealous.

'I can't swim in that tank,' said Felicity. 'I'm allergic to cat poo.'

'Don't be a wimp,' said The Boss. 'We have a show on soon. It will take all day to empty the water and fill it up again.'

'I am NOT swimming in polluted water,' she said. 'Never.'

I quietly picked up a net and scooped out the poo.

'Jack will have to go on,' said The Boss. 'He won't mind a bit of poo.'

'I don't let Jack swim any more,' said Felicity. 'You know that. He's past it.'

'Jack loves the water,' said The Boss. 'Don't be mean.'

Felicity thought for a bit. 'Okay,' she said. 'I'll go and get him.'

Felicity rushed off and came back with Jack. He was a tall man and he walked slowly and awkwardly. His skin was all shiny and quite shrivelled. He looked like a person who didn't want to live. I felt sorry for him.

And so did Singenpoo.
She had followed him back
from the van. She jumped
up straight into his
arms.

Yes. Singenpoo.
My cat. Singenpoo
never let *anyone*
pick her up
except me.

I couldn't
believe it. Why
was she going
to another
person? She
seemed to be
crazy about
Jack.

I didn't
like it. Not
one little bit.

Singenpoo was purring like mad. It was almost as if she was in love with Jack. I tried to push down my jealous feelings.

'I'm Scott,' I said to Jack.

The Boss laughed. 'Jack can't talk,' he said. 'He's never spoken a word in his whole life.'

The poor man just stared at the floor and held on tightly to Singenpoo. He looked like the unhappiest person in the whole world. But still and all. He wasn't going to get my cat. Singenpoo loved *me*.

'Okay, Jack,' said the Boss. 'You'll have to go on.'

Jack squeezed Singenpoo tightly to his chest. He jumped up and down clumsily. He wanted to do an act.

'We need your help,' said The Boss. 'The silly cat has fouled the water. Felicity won't swim in it.'

Felicity smiled at Jack. 'It's okay,' she said. 'Just this once. Go and put on your outfit.'

Jack gave a nod and hurried off towards their caravan, still carrying Singenpoo.

'Here, girl,' I said. 'Singenpoo. Puss, puss, puss.'

Singenpoo didn't come. She went with Jack.

She liked Jack better than me. Why? What had I done to upset her? What *was* it with Jack?

3

After about ten minutes Singenpoo came back. It was good to see her. I was starting to get worried. So was Felicity. 'Where's Jack gone?' she said.

Just at that moment Jack stumbled in. 'That is the worst outfit I have ever seen,' I whispered to The Boss.

'It's a bunyip outfit,' he said.

'A bunyip?' I yelped. 'There's no such thing.' It was crazy. No one would believe that Jack was a bunyip. The green fur was falling out and there were bald spots everywhere. The only bits that looked real were the webbed feet and hands. The face mask had green hair and funny eyes. Talk about weird.

'Okay,' said The Boss. 'The customers are lining up. Get into the tank, Jack.'

Jack climbed eagerly into the tank.

He plunged into the water with a big splash and started swimming around under water.

I tell you what. Jack couldn't talk. But he sure could swim. He was even better than The Mermaid. He was having a great time. Singenpoo couldn't take her eyes off the performance.

The Boss looked at me and Singenpoo. 'Okay,' he said. 'Now it's your turn to put on a show.'

'Come on, Singenpoo,' I said. 'We're on.' She didn't seem to want to come. I had to pick her up and carry her into our side-show tent. There was already a big crowd waiting to see her do her stuff.

I picked up the microphone and looked at the audience. I was very nervous. It was my first real day and I wanted to make a big impression. 'Ladies and gentlemen,' I said. 'Please welcome Singenpoo, the cat who can read.'

The people clapped politely. 'Not only can Singenpoo read,' I said. 'But she can write too.'

I could see people gasp and look at each other. They didn't believe it. I smiled at Singenpoo but she didn't seem to notice. I started to grow worried. Her mind was on something else. What if she refused to perform?

I took Singenpoo over to the computer and put her in front of the screen.

'Just call out a word,' I said to the audience. 'And Singenpoo will type it out.'

'Rhinoceros,' shouted a cheeky little kid in the front row. I nodded at Singenpoo nervously. Rhinoceros was a hard word.

Singenpoo started to tap on the keyboard. *Tap, tap, tap, tap.*

I stared at the screen. JACK. Singenpoo had typed the word JACK. Oh no. This was terrible.

Some people in the audience laughed. One person booed.

'Give them a go,' called a nice old lady.

'Someone else,' I said. 'Anyone. Give me another word.'

'Pig,' said the old lady.

Good, an easy word. I nodded at Singenpoo. But I could have saved my breath. She was tapping away already: IS A PRISONER.

What was this? JACK IS A PRISONER. Singenpoo had gone crazy. People started to boo and shout. Others were looking puzzled. But most thought we were phoneys.

'Fake.'

'Put-up job. It's a computer trick.'

'We want our money back.'

Singenpoo looked up at the angry mob. She was frightened.

'It's okay, girl,' I said. 'Settle down.'

But Singenpoo didn't settle down. She was terrified by all the yelling. She started to shake and meow. Suddenly she shot out of the tent and disappeared from sight.

The crowd was angry. People surged towards the EXIT waving their tickets, shouting and asking for a refund.

The Boss was upset. He wanted people to like his shows. 'Okay, okay,' he yelled. 'You can have your money back.'

This was bad. But worse was to come. More people were streaming out of Felicity's side-show tent. They were yelling and wanting their money back too. They didn't like Jack's bunyip act.

'What a rip-off,' said a bloke with a long beard.

'That is the worst outfit I have ever seen,' said a woman who was with him.

'Call that a bunyip?' said a mean-looking kid. 'Bunyips don't have ears like that. I want my money back.'

Both shows were total failures. The Boss had to give everyone a refund. He went off shaking his head and waving his arms at the sky.

I searched the ground with my eyes looking for Singenpoo. But she was nowhere to be seen.

Suddenly Felicity walked out of her tent dragging Jack behind her. It reminded me of a mother pulling a little kid along in the supermarket. Poor Jack stumbled and nearly fell. I guessed it must have been hard to walk in that hot, rubbery bunyip outfit.

'I knew you were past it,' she said sadly. 'I shouldn't have let you go on.'

'Singenpoo,' I called. 'Singenpoo. Where are you?' I searched high and low. I peered under caravans and inside every trailer. I pushed past the crowds and tried to shout over the roar of the stunt motorbikes. I even looked somewhere Singenpoo would never go – inside the juggling dog's tent. But there was nothing. Singenpoo had disappeared.

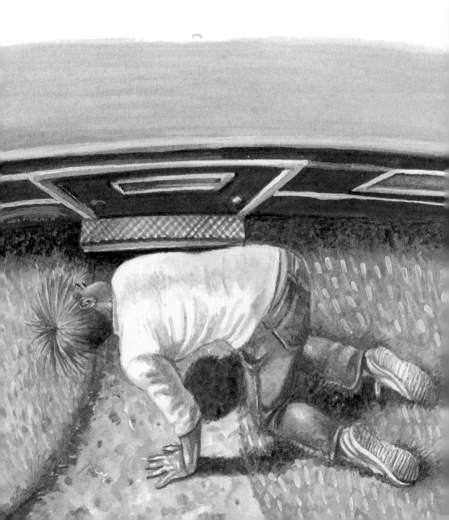

It was hopeless. I was really worried as I walked back to our caravan. Singenpoo was a very sensitive cat. She would have been upset by all the yelling. What if she had been hit by a dodgem car? Or stood on by the elephant?

I couldn't bear to think about it. It would be so lonely without Singenpoo.

'Where *are* you, girl?' I said to nobody. 'Please come home.'

I wished I had never seen this carnival. I didn't want the stupid job in a side-show any more. I would have to find another way of getting money for Mum. I didn't care whether Singenpoo read words or didn't read words. I just wanted her back. I loved her more than anything in the world. I thought about the way she curled up on my bed at night. I remembered how she licked ice-cream off my fingers with her rough tongue. She loved me more than anyone else.

Or did she? *Jack*. She was mad about Jack.

But she *couldn't* be with him. Could she? Not inside Felicity's caravan. She wouldn't have hidden in there. She'd *never* choose Jack over me. Would she?

I ran crazily towards Felicity's caravan, pushing my way through the crowd.

'Singenpoo, Singenpoo, Singenpoo,' I called out in desperation.

I reached the fake Mermaid's caravan and peered in through the windows. The van was empty. A number of rubber fish-tails hung from pegs on the wall. There were dishes in the sink and two unmade beds.

But there was no one there.

I rattled the door. It was still locked. So where was Jack?

That's when I noticed it. The air vent in the caravan roof. It was broken off. And the flywire had a big hole in it. Something sharp like a knife – or claws – had ripped a hole in the flywire.

Jack had escaped.

But where was Singenpoo? I had to find her. I tried to blink back the tears that were pricking my eyes.

I staggered back into the tent where Singenpoo had done her act. There was still no sign of her.

But the computer caught my eye.

I looked at the screen. Some new words had been written there:

DEAR SCOTT

I HAVE TO SAVE JACK. HE IS . . .

The message wasn't finished. But I knew who had written it. Singenpoo. And she must have left in a hurry. She *had* run away with Jack.

Jack couldn't look after her properly. He was too old and too doddery. At this very moment Singenpoo could be under the wheels of a truck. Or in the jaws of a dog.

Why had she done it? I knew the answer but I didn't want to face it. The truth was that she liked Jack better than me. She didn't want me any more.

I walked out of the tent in a daze. I had heard of cats going to live with someone else. Mrs Bridge, who lived next door to my mum, had a cat like that. Once Mrs Bridge had gone to hospital and come home with a new baby. That very day her cat had moved in with the people over the road. It wouldn't come back. Not for anything.

Now Singenpoo had gone off with Jack. After so long together. After all we'd been through. I was devastated.

'Jack's gone off with your cat,' said a voice. It was Felicity. Tears were streaming down her face. 'You should keep it locked up,' she said. 'It's a menace. If I get my hands on it I'll – '

I cut her off. 'Singenpoo can go where she likes,' I yelled. 'If she likes Jack better than me, well, she can go with him. You can't force a pet to love you.'

We both stared at each other, thinking about what I had just said. Would I really let Singenpoo go? Or would I rip her out of Jack's arms and lock her up in my bedroom? My mum wouldn't let *me* go off into danger. So why should I let Singenpoo leave? Even if she wanted to.

'The cat is a menace,' Felicity sobbed. 'If I catch it I'll teach it to stay away from my Jack. He was happy with me. The cat is leading him astray. He doesn't want to go. He's my Jack. Mine, mine, mine.'

Her voice grew loud and squeaky and her eyes flashed in a weird way. She started to rush all over the place looking under caravans and boxes.

Singenpoo was in danger. If Felicity caught up with her anything might happen. She seemed to have gone crazy. I rushed out of the carnival site and onto the road. Where were they? Where were the runaways? I had to find them before Felicity did.

4

I stared up the street. I stared down the street. Nothing. Not a sign... Hang on. Yes, yes. There was a sign. There on the footpath. An arrow. A wet arrow traced out on the ground. I bent down and touched it with the tip of one finger and sniffed. Yes. It was. Cat wee. And not just any cat wee. It was Singenpoo's, for sure. I would have known it anywhere.

Singenpoo wanted me to follow. She had written a sign the only way she could. What a relief.

What a cat.

I began to run along the road in the direction of the arrow. I came to a crossroad. Now which way? Where had they gone? Oh yes. Look. Another arrow pointing to the left. Singenpoo was leaving arrows at every turn. I hurried on. There was no time to waste. I was worried that the wee arrows would evaporate in the hot sun.

I followed the arrows through the town and out into the countryside. Where were the escapees heading? What were they up to? I had to catch them. At every turn or crossroad there was an arrow. But each time I found one it was smaller than the one before. Then I realised what was happening.

Singenpoo was running out of wee. I had to catch up. And fast. Before I lost them.

After another ten minutes I came to a fork in the road. There were no houses or people to be seen anywhere. And there was no arrow either.

I dropped down onto my knees and searched. There must be a sign somewhere. Yes, there was. One of the arrows, small and faint, was just drying out in the rays of the sun. I knew which way to go.

Something made me look back down the road. Someone was coming. A woman. Felicity was following us. She stopped and fell down onto her knees and sniffed at the road. She was following the arrows too. She wanted to find Jack and Singenpoo as much as I did.

Oh no. I had to do something. I had to throw her off the scent.

5

If Felicity reached the fork in the road she wouldn't know which way to go. But she had a fifty-fifty chance. She might take the correct fork and catch up with Singenpoo and Jack. If she got her hands on Singenpoo she might freak out.

What could I do?

There was only one thing.

I quickly pulled down the zip on my trousers. Then I made my own wet arrow on the road.

Pointing the wrong way.

I zipped up my fly and jumped into the bushes. Just in time. Felicity came charging up and stood staring down at my wet mark on the road. 'Ha,' she yelled. She made off in the wrong direction as quickly as she could go. Amazing. She couldn't even tell the difference between human pee and cat pee.

I waited until she was out of sight and quickly ran after Singenpoo and Jack. I had to catch up. I wasn't going to let Jack go off with my cat without trying to win her back. She was mine. And mine alone.

These were the thoughts that were in my mind as I ran along the deserted country road.

When the end came I wasn't ready for it.

No one would have been ready for what I saw around the next corner.

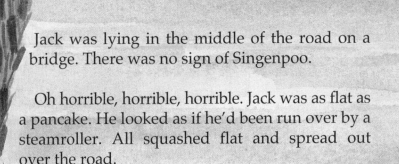

Jack was lying in the middle of the road on a bridge. There was no sign of Singenpoo.

Oh horrible, horrible, horrible. Jack was as flat as a pancake. He looked as if he'd been run over by a steamroller. All squashed flat and spread out over the road.

I walked slowly up to his flattened body. This was weird. This was crazy. His body was like an empty skin bag. And there were no eyes – only holes where they should have been.

Then I saw it.

A zip.

Jack's skin had a zip all the way down the back. This was crazy. How could a human body have a zip?

Suddenly I heard a meow.

It was Singenpoo. And… And… The Bunyip. The poor old Bunyip was swimming in the water-hole under the bridge. He was lying on his back happily squirting water up out of his mouth.

It hit me like a slammed door.

The Bunyip was real. And Jack was the fake. All these years The Bunyip must have been dressed up as a human. In a fake human skin.

6

The Bunyip swam quickly to the side of the waterhole and stepped out next to Singenpoo. Now his skin did not look ratty and old. It glistened green and blue and shiny. It reflected the clear sky above like a coat of clouds. The Bunyip was beautiful.

'Come back, come back,' cried a woman's voice.

It was Felicity. She came running up to us. Tears were streaming down her face. She stared down at The Bunyip and Singenpoo.

'Help me,' she sobbed. 'Stop him. He's all I've got.'

I couldn't believe that she wanted me to get The Bunyip back.

'Why did you keep him locked up?' I asked.

'I had to do it,' she said. 'I found his mother dead in the forest. Jack was only a baby in her pouch. So I took him home and kept it a secret. If anyone had known they would have put him in a zoo. Or gone looking for other bunyips and captured them.

'But Jack grew too big. People would have found out. They might have taken him away from me.'

'So you put him in a human suit?' I gasped. 'And pretended that The Bunyip was a fake?'

Felicity nodded. 'I only did it for him,' she sobbed. 'When he was a baby he loved being with me. But when he grew up he kept running away towards the forest – and the water.'

'And no one knew?' I asked.

'Only The Boss,' she answered. 'And your cat. It's so darn smart.'

53

I felt sorry for her. It must be awful to lose an animal that you love. If Singenpoo left I would never get over it.

'Come back,' she called again.

The Bunyip hesitated.
I could see that he loved
her too. But he wanted to
be free. To go back where
he belonged.

He shook his head at Felicity.
Then he skipped, ever so lightly,
to the edge of the forest. He was going to run off.

Singenpoo stared up at me. Then she looked at The Bunyip. She was going with him. I would never see her again. I opened my mouth to call out. To beg Singenpoo not to leave me.

But I didn't.

'It's all right, girl,' I said in a choked voice. 'Go if you want to.'

Singenpoo looked at me. Then she looked at The Bunyip. She took a few steps towards the forest. Then she turned and sped towards me.

54

She leapt into my arms.

I hugged her and hugged her and hugged her.
I kissed her black fur and her shiny wet nose.

Felicity was still crying as The Bunyip disappeared into the forest.

I patted her on the shoulder. 'He's happy,' I said. 'Bunyips belong in the bush. But cats don't.'

Felicity looked into the forest and smiled at what she heard. A happy, gurgling laugh echoed through the trees.

The Bunyip had gone home.

7

When we got back to the carnival
The Boss had bad news.

'I'm sorry, Scott,' he said. 'But the
crowds don't believe in a reading cat.
They think it's a computer trick. I can't
use you any more.'

I hung my head. We were out of work
again. Sacked.

'I think I'll leave too,' said Felicity sadly.
'Now that I don't have anyone to help me.'

Suddenly I brightened up. 'Wait a minute,'
I yelled.

'I've got an idea.'

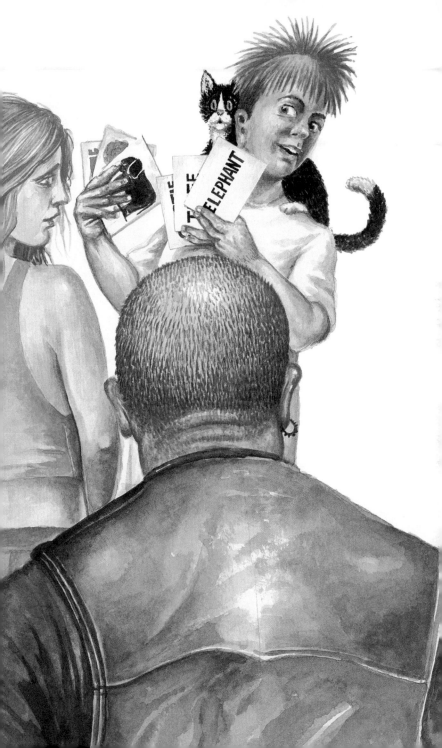

Singenpoo didn't like it at first. Cats don't like water because of the cold. So we bought her a wetsuit. And goggles.

And we all went into business together. She was the only cat in the world who could read and write underwater.

I didn't tell Felicity how Singenpoo kept herself warm. What she didn't know wouldn't hurt her.

And neither would a little bit of cat wee.

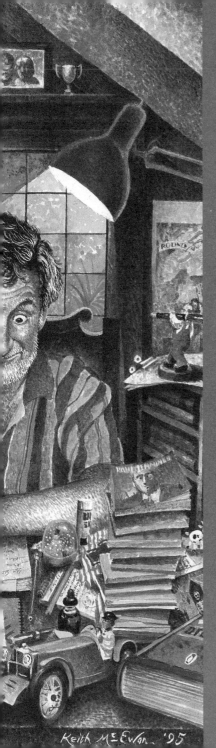

A word from Paul

I love writing stories about Singenpoo because pets are very special. We hate it when anything bad happens to them. And sometimes it does.

Once one of my kids had a pet duckling. It was taken by a fox while he was at school. He was only young and I knew that my son was going to be upset. I tried to find another duckling that looked the same but all that was available was one huge fully grown duck. I bought it and put it in the pen.

I waited sadly for my son to come home. I wasn't looking forward to telling him what had happened and wondered if he would like the replacement duck.

When he came home he raced up to the cage and grinned. 'Gee,' he said. 'She's grown a lot today.'

Sometimes you can be lucky.

Paul